Rapunzel Can

0 0567 77819

Rapunzel can run.
She can run with her feet.

Rapunzel can swing.
She can swing with her hair.

Rapunzel can sing.
She can sing with her voice.

Rapunzel can paint.
She can paint with her brush.

Rapunzel can knit.
She can knit with her needles

Rapunzel can play.
She can play with her friends.

What can you do?